What Are Friends For?

For David—S.G.

For Jackie—P.D.

KINGFISHER
Larousse Kingfisher Chambers Inc.
95 Madison Avenue
New York, New York 10016

First published in hardcover in 1998
First published in paperback in 2000
2 4 6 8 10 9 7 5 3 (HC)
2 4 6 8 10 9 7 5 3 1 (PB)

1TR/0400/WKT/RPR/ZKM157

LIBRARY OF CONGRESS CATALOGING-IN-PUBLICATION DATA
Grindley, Sally.
What are friends for? / Sally Grindley : illustrated by Penny Dann.
—1st ed.
p. cm.
Summary: Even when Figgy Twosocks makes Jefferson Bear cross, they
discover that a "friend is forever."
[1. Foxes—Fiction. 2. Bears—Fiction. 3. Friendship—Fiction.]
I. Dann, Penny, ill. II. Title.
PZ7.G88446Wf 1998
[E]—dc21 97-39699 CIP AC

ISBN 0-7534-5108-5 (HC)
ISBN 0-7534-5285-5 (PB)

Printed in Hong Kong/China

What Are Friends For?

Sally Grindley
Illustrated by Penny Dann

KINGfISHER

NEW YORK

Jefferson Bear and Figgy Twosocks went
walking one day in the sunny green woods.
"JB," asked Figgy Twosocks,
"are you my friend?"

"Yes," said Jefferson Bear.
"I am your friend, and you are my friend."
"But what is a friend for?" asked
Figgy Twosocks.
"Well…" said Jefferson Bear.
"A friend is for playing."

"Goody," said Figgy Twosocks. "Let's play hide-and-seek."

"All right," said Jefferson Bear. "You hide first."

Figgy Twosocks hid in a hollow tree.

Jefferson Bear looked everywhere,

but couldn't find her.

When it was his turn,
he hid behind a tree stump.
Figgy Twosocks
found him straightaway.
"You're better at this
than me," said
Jefferson Bear.

"I'll help you this time,"
said Figgy Twosocks. She hid
under a pile of leaves,
but left the tip of her
tail showing.

The next day, Figgy Twosocks asked, "JB, what else is a friend for?"

"Well," said Jefferson Bear, scratching his head. "A friend is for sharing."

"We share, don't we, JB? We share the sky and the hills and the trees."

"Yes," said Jefferson Bear, "we share lots of things."

"What do *best* friends share?" asked Figgy Twosocks.

"Well," said Jefferson Bear,
"best friends share their favorite things."
Figgy Twosocks thought about this, then darted
into the woods. When she came back, she was
tugging an enormous
bramble covered with
blackberries.

"Would you like some, JB?"
she said. "Blackberries
are my favorites.
Yummy, aren't they?"

"De–licious," said Jefferson Bear.

That afternoon, loud squeals woke
Jefferson Bear from his sleep.

yelp! *yelp!* *yelp!* *yelp!*

yelp! yelp! yelp! yelp!

"I'm coming," he bellowed.
"What's the matter?"

He found Figgy Twosocks lying on the ground.

"You've got a thorn in your foot. Hold still and I'll take it out."

"Will it hurt?" whimpered Figgy Twosocks.

"I'll be as gentle as I can," said Jefferson Bear.

Figgy Twosocks was frightened when she saw her friend's sharp teeth, but she lay still. Jefferson Bear closed his teeth around the thorn and pulled.

As soon as it was out, Figgy Twosocks jumped up and pranced around.

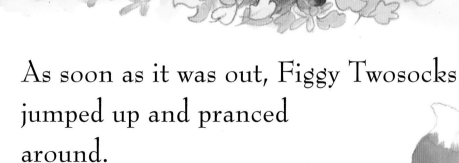

"Thank you, JB," she said.
"Thank you for helping me."
"That's what friends are for,"
said Jefferson Bear.

T he next afternoon, Jefferson Bear was dozing in the sun. Figgy Twosocks wanted to play. She crept up behind him and yelled…

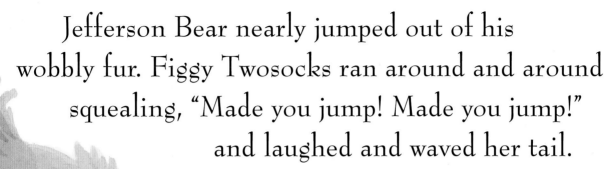

Jefferson Bear nearly jumped out of his
wobbly fur. Figgy Twosocks ran around and around
squealing, "Made you jump! Made you jump!"
and laughed and waved her tail.

Jefferson Bear
didn't think it was funny.

"Go away, Figgy Twosocks," he said.
"You have made me cross."

"But I want to play," said Figgy Twosocks.

"And I want to sleep," said Jefferson Bear.
"A big brown bear needs his sleep."

"And a little red fox needs her play,"
said Figgy Twosocks.

"Then go and play somewhere else,"
said Jefferson Bear.

"You're not my friend anymore," said
Figgy Twosocks sadly, and she trudged off.

W hen Jefferson Bear woke up the next morning, he felt sorry that he had upset his friend.

"I'll play with her today," he said to himself.

But Figgy Twosocks stayed away.

Jefferson Bear began to worry. He went to her den and called, "Figgy Twosocks, it's Jefferson Bear.
Are you all right?"

There was no reply.

Jefferson Bear's worry grew. He walked to
the edge of the river and called again,
"Where are you, Figgy Twosocks?"

But there was no reply.

Jefferson Bear's worry grew bigger. He walked through the woods calling, "Come out, Figgy Twosocks, it's me, Jefferson Bear."

But there was still no reply.

At last, he came to the hollow tree where they had played hide-and-seek. He saw the tip of a tail sticking out.

"Figgy Twosocks, is that you?" he called. "It's JB."

He listened and thought
he heard something.

He listened again and was
sure he heard a sniff.

The sniff grew
louder and
louder and louder
until it turned
into a **great**

big

SOB.

"Figgy Twosocks?" said Jefferson Bear.

"Yes," sobbed Figgy Twosocks.

"Please come out," said Jefferson Bear.
"I miss you."

"I'm sorry, JB," said Figgy Twosocks.
"I didn't mean to make you cross."

"And I'm sorry I was so grumpy,"
said Jefferson Bear. "Let's go and play."

"JB," sniffed Figgy Twosocks,
"does that mean you're still my friend?"

"Of course I'm still your friend,"
said Jefferson Bear. "A friend is forever."